E
AL

Allen, Pamela

Who sank the boat?

DATE DUE

NO 30 '87	MR 19 '91	JUN 30 '94	APR 24 '96
JY 07 '88	NO 8 '91	JUL 21 '94	JUL 25 '96
JA 19 '89	FE 10 '92	AUG 16 '94	OCT 15 '96
MY 22 '89	'92	NOV 28 '94	NOV 07 '96
JY 20 '89	MY 27 '93	02 95	FEB 10 '97
MR 9 '90	JY 15 '93	MAR 02 95	JUN 05 '97
JE 25 '90	OC 28 '93	MAR 24	JUL 29 '97
AG 21 '90	DEC 6 '93	JUL 13 '95	AUG 08 '97
AG 27 '90	DEC 28 '93	JUL 20 '95	

DEMCO 25-380

© THE BAKER & TAYLOR CO.

Who Sank the Boat?

To my mother
Esma Griffiths

Copyright © 1982 by Pamela Allen
First American Edition 1983
First printing
Printed in the United States of America
All rights reserved. This book, or parts thereof,
may not be reproduced in any form without permission
in writing from the publishers.
First published by Thomas Nelson Australia
Library of Congress Cataloging in Publication Data
Allen, Pamela.   Who sank the boat?
Summary: The reader is invited to guess who
causes the boat to sink when five animal friends
of varying sizes decide to go for a row.
[1. Animals — Fiction.   2. Boats and boating —
Fiction]   I. Title.
PZ7.A433Wh 1983   [E]   82-19832
ISBN 0-698-20576-6

Who Sank the Boat?

Pamela Allen

Coward–McCann, Inc.   New York

Beside the sea, on Mr Peffer's place,
there lived

a cow, a donkey, a sheep, a pig,
and a tiny little mouse.

They were good friends,
and one warm sunny morning,
for no particular reason,
they decided to go
for a row in the bay.

Do you know who sank the boat?

Was it the cow
who almost fell in,
when she tilted the boat
and made such a din?

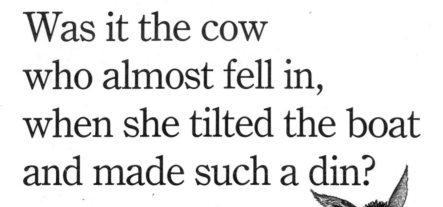

No, it wasn't the cow
who almost fell in.

Do you know who sank the boat?

Was it the donkey
who balanced her weight?
Who yelled,
'I'll get in at the bow before it's too late.'

No, it wasn't the donkey
who balanced her weight.

Do you know who sank the boat?

Was it the pig
as fat as butter,
who stepped in at the side
and caused a great flutter?

No, it wasn't the pig
as fat as butter.

Do you know who sank the boat?

Was it the sheep
who knew where to sit
to level the boat
so that she could knit?

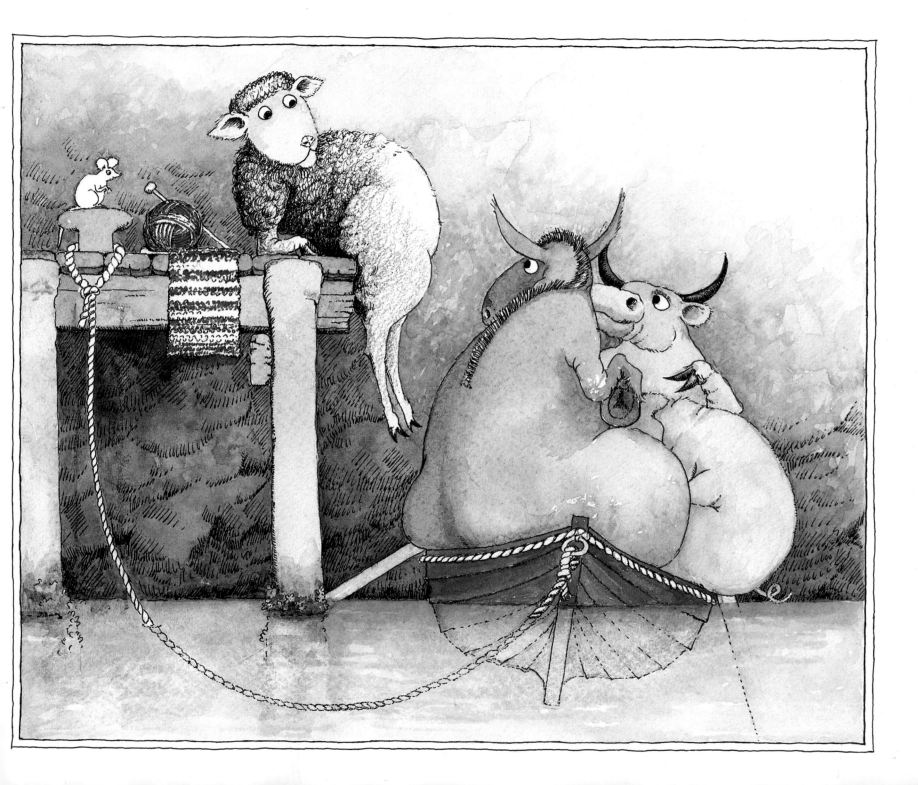

No, it wasn't the sheep
who knew where to sit.

Do you know who sank the boat?

Was it the little mouse,
the last to get in,
who was lightest of all?

Could it be him?

You DO know who sank the boat.